Inheritance

David Reynolds-Moreton

sci-fi-cafe.com

sci-fi-cafe.com

CHAPTER 1

BODE AWOKE FROM a deep and untroubled sleep in his night chamber deep inside the cliff as the sunlight burst through onto his face. The light entered through a hole high up on the cliff wall and reflected from several mirrors of polished metal set in tunnels laboriously cut many generations ago to reach deep into the huge outcrop of rock.

He peeled back his bed covering and reached out for his light jar, giving it a good shaking to liven up the beetles within. As the little brown creatures rattled around in the jar, they began to give out their natural green glow, softly lighting up the chamber.

When the light was strong enough, Bode went over to the wooden plug set in the wall of his sleeping chamber which held back the water in the bathing area, and let the cool cleansing gush wash the final traces of sleep from his body. He then opened the jar and dropped in a couple of gig tree leaves on which the beetles would feed, so gaining energy to provide him with light when he retired that evening.

Bode had decided to try and get some more of the light beetles, but they were hard to find, and the transparent casing in which they were kept took a lot of work to make. The horn of the kepper bull was boiled for several hours until the outer layer was soft enough to peel away, and the soft inter layer was then moulded to form a jar shape. When dried, it became transparent and hard, an ideal home for the light emitting beetles; but getting the horn in the first place was not without its dangers.

His home consisted of several cave-like rooms interlinked by short tunnels cut in the rock, and had been handed down to him from an old man who said he was his father. He doubted that as he had no recollection of any parents - he just was, and always had been, as far as he could remember.

He went down a side tunnel to the dark room where he grew his main crop of food plants. They were strange plants, only growing in total darkness, unlike all other plants which needed the bright light of the greater sun to make them grow. Bode slid a small wooden window covering to one side to let in enough light for him to see the plants, and selecting a young soft stem, he cut it off at the base, returned the shutter to its closed position and went into the main chamber to prepare his morning meal.

He carefully stripped the outer covering off the stem, and then chopped the soft juicy core into small pieces, placing them in his wooden eating bowl. A quick sprinkle of powder from the dried bando fruit, and he was ready to break his night-time fast.

Today he would go to the forbidden zone to retrieve some more of the shiny metal pieces which could be found there, as he needed to add a few more mirrors to take the light further into his cave complex.

He never did understand why they were not allowed to go into certain areas; he had asked some of the older members of the group, but they just said it had always been so, and no one should go there. If he was caught, he could well be expelled from the group, although that didn't really bother him much as they were a useless bunch anyway, and did little to better their lot in life.

He finished his meal with a round bun made from ground felix seed, which had been baked in the tiny oven at the back of the room some few days before. Once baked, the buns would keep for many days, unlike the buns the others made which sprouted a green mould like fur after only a few hours. He had tried to get the others to try his method, but they just said that was how they had always done it, and he shouldn't mess with tradition.

Bode washed his bowl out, swept the crumbs off the table and got ready for his journey into the forbidden lands. A long blade of metal was taken off the wall, the edge tested for sharpness, and then slung onto the belt he always wore around his waist. Two water gourds and eight seed buns would sustain him for most of the journey, these were placed in a woven bag and attached to the belt. They would be supplemented with wild fruit and nuts as he travelled. Just before he left, he added a piece of smoulder wood to the embers of the fire in the back wall of the chamber, picked up his walking stave and then went to the massive wooden entrance door of his home; Bode hadn't made the door, it had been there when he took the cave system over from his supposed father, but he had added the camouflage which made it difficult to find if you didn't know where to look.

Someone from the village clan had said there was a new large animal roaming the area; Bode hadn't seen it, but was told it had killed two people from the next village, and they were afraid to go out unless in a large group armed with spears; he was tempted to dismiss it as just another wild story from someone's imagination, but he would be just that little bit more careful when going out alone.

There had been stories of a marauding gang of travellers who took anything they could get their hands on, and as his home was some distance from the rest of the settlement, he thought it wise to conceal it in some way. Quite by chance, Bode had discovered that the juice obtained when boiling the stems of the jackle plant made very good glue. He had woven a piece of coarse cloth the size of the door, soaked it in the glue and stuck it onto the door. While still wet, he had then sprinkled on some ground up rock from the cliff wall - when viewed from a short distance the doorway had blended into the cliff, and was almost invisible.

Closing the door behind him and inserting the lock stick, Bode strode purposefully off on his long journey to the forbidden lands. Not wishing to give away his intentions to any of his clan who might be wandering around the area, he turned left and up the steep sided valley leading to the bubbling mud pools, few people ever went there.

Some said that the mud pools were the resting place of a group of people who had displeased the Gods, and had been drowned for their sins; the bubbles were from the breath of the people entrapped there, and if you got too close, they could drag you in. He didn't believe it for one moment, but always trod carefully around the pools just in case he slipped in.

It was only safe to go up the valley in the early morning or late evening, as flying insects, about the size of a closed fist lived there. During the day they could be seen buzzing around looking for whatever they ate, but during the darker hours they returned to their nests high up in the valley walls, and it was safer to go up the valley then. Although he had never been stung, it was said that if they stung you, the unfortunate recipient of such a sting would go into a deep sleep for several days, and the sting left a large painful bump which took many days to disperse.

One thing the insects didn't like was smoke, so Bode collected up some dry grass and bound it onto a small branch pulled from a nearby shrub. Using his fire making stick, he struck some sparks onto the bundle, and gently blew onto the tiny flame until a goodly portion of the bundle was alight. He then smothered the bundle in some green grass until the flames went out, leaving him with a smoking lump of grass on the end of the branch.

As Bode went up the valley, the sides got higher and the pathway became narrow; in some places he could almost touch the walls with outstretched arms, not that he would do so in case something unpleasant was lurking in the many holes dotted about in the valley walls. Looking up, he could see a few of the flying insects they all dreaded, buzzing around, looking for their hiding holes for the daylight hours.

He often wondered why there were so many dangerous creatures around in his otherwise peaceful world - what purpose did they serve? Why were they there? When he had asked the elders they had just shrugged, and said it had always been so, and was possibly a punishment for past sins. He didn't believe that either.

At the end of the valley there was one more hazard to confront - the sticky vines. They hung down from the jumble of rocks above, and if you touched them you could be trapped. He had been told that if you pulled away from the sticky surface, they tended to wrap around whatever they had touched, and eventually you would be slowly pulled up into the rocks - what happened then no one knew, but speculation left little to the imagination. There was only one thing to be done, and that was to cut down enough of the dangling ends in order to let one pass.

Bode drew his cutting blade and very carefully sliced off the ends which impeded his progress, his nose wrinkling up at the unpleasant smell the vines exuded, and then he was through to the end of the valley. Looking back, he could see the slime dripping from the severed ends of the vines, knowing full well they would have grown back in a couple of days and would have to be removed again.

As the steep sides of the valley dropped away, Bode found himself in the deep depression of the mud pools. He would have to make his way between them as there was no way around because the whole area was surrounded by sharp and jumbled rocks. Quite by accident, he had discovered that the mud from the pools was very useful for polishing to a brilliant finish the metal he had salvaged from the forbidden lands, and these pieces of metal then became the mirrors which spread light into the cave complex.

By another happy accident, he also discovered another feature of the stinking mud; when polishing his mirrors he found the block of mud had dried out, and he had to re-mix it to a smooth paste using a piece of stick in a gourd. Having got the mud to the right consistency he threw the mixing stick with its blob of mud on the end into his fire, and next morning he noticed the blob of mud had turned into a hard substance which would not soften with water. It was like a little cup, the stick having burnt away.

Bode often wondered why his clan believed so fervently in the unlikely stories they told, and the mud pools were no exception. He knew instinctively that a person couldn't survive below the bubbling mud, as he had nearly drowned in a water pool some years ago, but he did wonder why the mud bubbled as it did. Carefully he stepped between the seething mud pools, but as the ground beneath his feet gave way a little to his body weight, so he increased his speed just a bit, but not enough to cause him to lose his balance as he swerved between the stinking pools. Why did the gas bubbles smell so awful? If people really were down there, they must all suffer from very bad breath, he concluded.

And another thing, he thought to himself as he strode out onto the smooth sand and gravel of the wastelands, what about the God they all seemed to believe in? Every seven days, and that seemed to be a significant number to the clan, they gave up a goodly portion of what they had gathered or made, to the God - or to be more precise, they threw it down a large smoking hole in the ground near their village, chanting some unintelligible words. He sometimes wondered if the clan leaders had a secret tunnel leading to the smoke hole, and gathered up the offerings for themselves - it was just an idea, but no more preposterous than some of the things they believed in. And where was this God? He had never seen a sign of it, nor did it answer any of the requests made by the clan.

Just ahead of him, Bode could see the outskirts of the forest which stretched right across the horizon. He would have to go through it, but it was risky - probably why none of the others would go near it.

There were poisonous plants, which would bring out a terrible rash if one was unfortunate or careless enough to brush up against them; another variety of the sticky vines, except they weren't sticky, but made up for the lack of stickiness by having tiny barbs along their length, and the power to pull one off ones feet if they managed to get a grip. He remembered seeing a small animal so caught, as it was whisked up into the branches above, and out of sight. And then there were the sleeping flowers, not that they slept, but if one were to smell their sweet scent for too long, you did. At the foot of any tree from which they hung, there would be a pile of small bones - all that was left after the sleeping flowers had done their magic, but the bones were small, so perhaps they were not powerful enough to devour him - but he wouldn't be taking any chances.

Many and varied were the threats in the forest, but if he wanted the shiny metal from the forbidden lands beyond, he would have to go through the forest and out the other side.

Bode trod carefully between the hanging vines and only had a couple of sniffs of the heady perfume from the sleeping flowers as he passed beneath them, and then he stopped dead in his tracks. Ahead was a metre long caterpillar-like thing with a tuft of spiny hairs under its chin, humping its way across the clearing - and it stopped as well. A lone vine he hadn't spotted slowly uncurled itself from above, just in front of the caterpillar's head, and swung in towards it. Before the vine could make contact, the caterpillar's head reared up, and from beneath its mouthpiece a single spiny hair shot out to bury itself in the vine. The reaction was instant - the vine curled up into the branches above so fast that Bode only just managed to catch a glimpse of it - and he thought he heard a faint squeal from above. The caterpillar lowered its head and continued its way across the clearing and out of sight beneath a clump of bushes.

Bode continued on his way, guided by the odd glimpse of the greater sun every now and again as the beams of light found their way through the thick canopy above to light up the forest floor in a dazzling blaze of colour. Beneath the mighty trees, the forest floor was covered with a green springy moss-like growth which Bode prodded with his stave as he went along.

Once, a long time ago, he had been in the forest and the moss had given way beneath his feet, one leg going down into a hole almost up to his knee. When he withdrew it, it was covered in tiny pale worm-like things, and he had a blistered and painful leg for several days. Bode came across the occasional rock in the forest on which he rested on his long hike, he didn't like to stand still in any one place for too long - just in case something under the moss considered his feet edible. Keep moving was his motto, staying in one place for too long was dangerous.

One of the strangest things he found in the dense forest was the jelly blob, as he referred to it. It was about half a metre high, pale amber in colour and translucent, although internal details were not visible, that's if there were any. It just sat there, unmoving, with a small ring of bare earth around its base as if nothing wanted to grow close to it. The outer surface looked as if it was wet, but he was reluctant to touch it to see if it really was, as he had no idea what the reaction would be. He had passed several jelly blobs today, and they all looked the same - they always did, but what did they feed on? All things ate something to sustain themselves, but the jelly blobs were a real mystery as he had never seen them catch anything.

As the greater sun began to sink and the light level dropped, he increased his pace to reach the rock he usually spent the night on when he went through the forest. It was difficult to climb, which made it an ideal place to rest as other creatures would find it hard to reach him - and none had succeeded so far.

As Bode neared his chosen spot for the night, he keep a lookout for fruit and nuts he recognised as edible, gathering them as he went along.

At last his haven came into sight in a small clearing, and he began the difficult climb to reach the top. At ten metres above the forest floor, Bode felt safe from predators, and there were no vines hanging down from above. A small depression in the top of the rock always contained a useful water supply, supplementing his drinking gourds - he would need them when he went through the hot zone.

Having lit a small fire from the dead wood he had gathered just before the climb, he settled down and made himself as comfortable as possible on the hard rock, and then he tucked in to the fruit and a bun from his supply.

As he was about to lay down for the nights sleep time, the lesser sun rose up above the trees, the silvery light shining down to bathe the clearing and his rocky perch in its ghostly glow.

CHAPTER 2

IN THE EARLY hours of the morning a blood curdling scream woke him up as something down below in the clearing was busily converting something else into a meal, and was being very noisy about it.

So far, while on his rock, he had never been attacked by the flying creatures which he knew inhabited the forest, and wondered why. Did the rock have something about it which repelled them? Or was it the pale light of the lesser sun which made flying difficult during the night hours? He knew they usually stayed high up it the tree tops, but he had seen them lower down on occasions.

Bode was fascinated by the lesser sun. It gave a little light but no heat, and had the suggestions of a face on it sometimes. What was it really? And why did it change shape? He had tried asking the clan elders, but only got the usual shrug and the standard answer of 'It's always been so,' which was no answer at all to his way of thinking.

Bode drifted back into a deep and peaceful sleep until the greater sun's light burst through the canopy to herald a new day. A few nuts and some fruit served as his morning meal, keeping the buns for when there might be no fruit to gather.

Climbing down was always more difficult than going up, but he reached the ground without mishap, and set off towards the forest's edge. As the massive trees of the forest began to thin out to be replaced with shrubs and bushes, Bode restocked his food bag, knowing such things would be scarce later on, especially in the hot zone.

Soon, he was out in the blazing light of the greater sun as it began to climb higher in the sky, and the plants grew shorter and in strange shapes here - long gone was the nice soft moss of the forest under his feet, it was now sand, gravel, and stones. In the distance he could see the next barrier on his journey.

Bode gathered up all the dried plant material he could find, and bound it into a bundle on the end of a couple of sticks; he knew what was ahead, and dreaded it, although he didn't know why - and that worried him. Things which couldn't be explained always did.

From where he stood it looked as if the whole world had split in half, and the section in front of him had risen up some hundred meters or so. It was a sheer cliff of black rock with wisps of pale smoke rising up here and there from small holes in the vertical surface. As he drew nearer to the formidable cliff, the plants grew smaller and less frequent, until there were no plants at all, just the bare ground.

The forest he knew about, and its dangers he knew how to avoid, but this place was different in some indiscernible way - it was dead, not just dead, but he felt it wanted to suck the very life out of him. There were no dangers here that he could see, but he still felt a dreadful fear - perhaps it was the fear of not knowing what he was afraid of.

As Bode approached the massive cliff he could hear the murmur of the voices, at least that's what it sounded like. It was like the low whispering of many people in distress - there were no clear words, just the moaning sounds, and feeling of torment and hopelessness. He had never seen anyone here, and there were no sign of bones or anything to denote the presence of anyone - but he felt as though there had been, at some time in the past.

Against the black of the cliff there was another even deeper blackness, the entrance he must go into, and the long tunnel which wound its way up to the top of the huge cliff. Bode lit one of his torches with his fire stick, and when it was blazing well, entered the hole. At first there was a total silence, a deadness - even his footsteps made no sound; a few metres further on and then the moaning returned. He felt a shiver go down his back, and the short stubby hairs on his head rose up like a bristle brush.

The flickering light from his torch lit up the jagged walls of the tunnel. To him it looked as if some mighty hand had ripped the rock out in great haste to form the tunnel, and not bothered to finish the job properly, although the floor was reasonably smooth. The air was hot, dusty and had a most unpleasant metallic smell about it, rather like when he once experienced when heating a piece of metal red hot, and hammering it out to make a ladle some time ago. Every so often, a small side passage would show up, but he didn't investigate any of them now. He had once been tempted to go down one passage which had a dull red glow in it, only to find a red hot boiling pool of something molten at its end, and he got his hair singed for his troubles as a gush of hot gas erupted from the pool and engulfed him for a moment.

There was one small passage near the top of the tunnel he always went down leading to a huge cave, the most beautiful thing he had ever seen, and he would do so again when he came to it. But first he had to negotiate the bridge. He called it that because it reminded him of a huge tree near his home which spanned a small river, and he had to cross it to reach some fruit trees which bore the most delicious fruit he had ever tasted. He often wondered why none of the others went across it, but they didn't, so he was able to trade things for the fruit from the other side.

The bridge was a narrow slab of rock which spanned a yawning chasm, at the bottom of which he could just see something red writhing about and bubbling. Once he had purposely carried in a large piece of wood and dropped it down the chasm when half way across the bridge, just to see what would happen. The wood hit the lurid surface and promptly burst into flames, lighting up the bottom of the boiling lava pit - reminding him of what would happen if he should fall in.

The torch was burning low as he reached the small tunnel, but he took a chance and entered.

The cave was big, very big, and full of huge white, transparent crystals, much bigger than he was. The flickering light from his torch lit up the crystals which sparkled with a life of their own as the light danced from one to another. He felt he could stay here all day, watching the ever changing light display, but he would need many torches to do so. With one last wistful look, Bode turned and left the cave as the torch was nearing the end of its life, and he still had a few tens of metres to go before he reached the open air above the cliff.

With a puff of smoke, the torch flame went out, and he could just see the glimmer of light ahead. Fortunately, this section of the tunnel held no hazards, so he just headed for the daylight.

Breathing deeply to clear his lungs of the hot and smelly air of the tunnel, he laid the spare torch near the entrance for the return journey, and turned to head out across the rolling sand dunes using the sun as his guide. This was the hot zone, and he would have to be careful not to drink too much of his water supply, as there was none to be had in this area - the next water he would encounter was on the fringe of the forbidden lands.

As the sun began to sink in a blaze of red, orange, and yellow, the first sign of the never ending dunes came into sight - a line of small trees, most of which he remembered bore fruit, so he could have a good feast before retiring for the dark hours, but first he must find water - his throat felt like a dried colig skin, which had been left out in the sun for several days. Where things grew, he knew water must be near, so he began to dig a hole near one of the biggest trees. Soon he hit damp earth, and then the hole began to full with water - a bit muddy, but it cleared as he scooped out the dirty water, returning it near the roots of the next tree.

A long time ago he had discovered that if the top of a gourd was cut off and scooped out, and the gourd left soaking in water for a while, it could be filled with water, placed on a fire and brought to the boil without the gourd catching fire, so making a hot herbal drink. Once he had refilled his water gourds with clean water, the pot gourd was left to soak as he hunted around for firewood. A curved line of three small trees with bushes between them would serve as a sleeping place for the night, and the fire would keep any nocturnal animals at bay, should there be any - not that he had ever seen any on previous visits.

With the fire burning merrily, and his pot gourd placed thereon full of water and a few herb leaves, he ate his evening meal of fruit and a bun, which had gone a bit hard, but the hot drink would make up for the extra effort of grinding the bun into submission. Finally, the stars came out, dusting the heavens with brilliant pinpoints of glittering diamonds, and then the lesser sun arose, bathing the scene in an unearthly silver light. It was time to sleep and let his tired muscles recover for the next day - a journey into the forbidden land itself, and the wonders it held.

Bode was up early next morning just as the stars were fading, and headed for the cleft in a huge ridge of rocks which swept across the horizon. It was the only way through to the forbidden lands that had been discovered, as far as he knew, and it was a steep climb, together with a few hazards. The main problem was the snakes, hundreds of them, very large, tiny and all sizes in between. They came out to warm themselves as soon as the greater sun arose, so he must get through the cleft before that happened. He had heard tales of those who had tried to go through during the day, and died a horrible death - and according to the tales, some had been swallowed whole.

Bode scrabbled down the last of the rocks and out onto the open plain as the greater sun arose in all its glory, bathing the world in bright light and very welcome warmth. Ahead, he could see the spires of the giant's dwellings, tall spindly things which reached up into the sky, although most had been reduced to rubble.

He had listened, fascinated, to tales of the giants; how they travelled around in boxes on wheels at great speed, far greater than a man could run, and how they had rods of metal which could kill an animal or a man at a great distance. One tale, which no one really gave any credence to, was about a flying thing which held hundreds of people and could fly all around the world; but a thing that big couldn't flap its wings, only birds could do that - and they were small.

Bode often wondered how these tales got started; there must be a bit of truth in them surely? Who could make up such things from their imagination, and pass them down through the generations? No

- there must have been a starting point for them, and maybe these strange things had happened, a very long time ago.

Most pathways were just earth where the grass had been flattened by many passing feet, but sometimes flat stones had been laid out where it would otherwise have been muddy - but here, in the land of the giants, pathways, or what was left of them, was of a hard smooth black stuff, which had a pleasant smell when warmed up by the sun on a very hot day. Bode came to the first of these strange pathways, and walked along it towards the piles of rubble which, he thought, must have been the homes of the giants.

They were not giants really, only about twice the height of men today, as he reasoned by comparing things of theirs which were similar to those he had seen in his world, although there were not many of them. The first few piles of rubble had been gone through for metal on earlier visits, so he strode on, through a flat area free of broken buildings to the first construction of the giants which didn't look too damaged.

It was made of stone, he was sure of that, but what kind of stone? It wasn't made of single blocks as a few of his clans buildings were, but one solid single block, with no joins showing. How could they have done this? If it had been cut from one big stone, how had they moved it to where it was now? Bode was in awe of the power the giants must have had to make such a thing. He walked around the building, looking for a way inside, and then he found it. It wasn't too unlike the door to his cave, except it was much bigger and possibly made of metal - it certainly wasn't wood, as it rang when he hit it with a stone.

On one side of the door there was what looked like an opening device with a handle. He tried moving it up and down, but it seemed stuck no matter how hard he tried, but just below the handle was a square section with a hole in it. The plastic covering had long ago melted off and dribbled down the door like a dark stain revealing the inner working of the electronic door lock. He looked around for something which he could poke into the hole, and found a metal rod lying on the ground. Picking it up, he rammed it into the hole and wriggled it around, and suddenly there was a loud click and the door moved a fraction.

He tried the handle again, and this time it moved in a downwards direction, and the door opened a few centimetres. With one almighty tug, the door swung open, and he was looking into the dark interior of one of the giants' buildings. Bode stepped inside, but he had to wait a while for his eyes to get accustomed to the low light level, and then he saw what the world of the giants was really like. Metal shutters must have adorned the windows at some time, but now they had been forced partly open by whatever had been the demise of the giants, and a little light seeped inside.

Bode was in a long hallway with doors on either side. He tried one, and it opened to a room of huge proportions, in the middle of which was a massive table with equally large chairs surrounding it, and the table had been laid out for a meal, as the plates and cutlery were still upon it. Scattered around the table, some on the chairs, but mostly on the floor, were the bones off the long gone giants, gleaming large and white in the soft light.

Bode felt a shudder run down his back as he surveyed the scene, it only needed the bodies to be clad in flesh, and he would have been back in the time of the giants. On the walls were somewhat faded pictures of people, country scenes, and odd looking machines, including one of the strange flying things he had heard about in the tales. He knew it was a flying machine, as it was clearly up in the clouds with the ground showing way down below. So some of the tales were true! What else in the old legends was also true? He shuddered again at the thought.

Bode left the dining room and went down the corridor to the next door, and opened it. This room was different; there were large chairs dotted about, a table, and the walls were covered in shelves in which were the remains of the family's collection of books. Bode took one down, being very careful not to let the decaying pages flutter to the floor, as the binding had rotted. His clan had a means of writing, albeit in picture form to represent things which were familiar to all, but these writings were very strange - little groups of symbols strung out in lines covered the pages, interspersed with the occasional picture. He carefully placed the book back on the shelf, wishing he could understand the strange markings as he felt it would tell him so much about the giants.

Once more out in the corridor, he tried another door which opened easily, and saw a flight of stairs leading up to the next level; the temptation was too much. It was hard work climbing the huge stairs, but he got to the top, a bit out of breath, but feeling it would be worth it. This part of the building had taken a hammering from whatever had destroyed the rest of the town, the windows had been blown in and a large hole in the flat roof had allowed wind-blown debris to pile up. He thought this was the sleeping and washing quarters from the broken remains of what looked like beds, but there was little else up here which made any sense to him.

Returning to the ground floor, Bode continued to search all the rooms which would open to him, and found one which tied in with another of the stories he had heard. Along one wall was a rack containing what looked like the metal rods which killed at a distance. He took one down, blew off the dust, and inspected it carefully. The metal rod was fixed to a wooden piece at one end, and below that a curved metal shape covered a little lever. He was tempted to work the lever, but thought it better to take it outside as he didn't know what would happen if he did.

Bode found a large metal box in one corner of the room and lifted the lid. It seemed to be full of tools, although he didn't know what some of them were used for - but he did recognise two saws, one of which had a fine blade, and he thought it might be for cutting metal. These were added to his carry bag.

There were many more strange things in the room, but not knowing their purpose, he left them alone. Bode left the gunroom, but took the rifle with him to see what would happen if he tried to use it. On his way out, he collected up a selection of the knives, forks, and spoons, as they were much better than any he or the others had, and placed then in his carry bag.

Once outside the building, he examined the rifle again. The metal rod had a hole in the end, so he assumed something would come out of it and do the killing, and it looked as if the little lever with the guard around it would make it work. He then noticed the front and rear sights, and reasoned this was what was used to point the rifle at the target. To use the sights he had to lift the rifle up to his shoulder to look through them, and then realised this was how one should hold the killing rod, but it was heavy and wobbled about a bit.

But what to aim at? There no animals around, in fact the whole area was devoid of life, so how would he know if it did kill? About twenty metres away an old street sign hung at an angle from its post, so he carefully lined the sights up on the middle of it, and squeezed the little lever.

A sharp crack made his ears hurt, but not as much as his shoulder as the rifle slammed back into it, leaving a nasty bruise. The street sign now had a neat hole in the middle of it, and his ears were still ringing. The rifle had automatically ejected the empty shell case, and Bode picked it up, surprised as it was still warm from the explosion.

Looking at the end of the case, he noticed the hole - so something must have come out of it - and that something had made a hole in the sign. Another close examination of the rifle, and he found the ammunition clip - and pulled it out.

The shells inside looked different to the one he had picked up, so the bit on the end was what flew out, he reasoned. But the rod would be useless when he had used up all the little tubes inside the clip. Back inside the gunroom, he rummaged around looking for another ammunition clip, but there were none, and then he spotted the boxes of shells, and an empty clip. The box disintegrated as he picked it up, the shells spilling out on the floor. It didn't take him long to load the clip, looking at the one he had removed from the rifle to make sure he got them the right way around.

Bode scooped up the rest of the spilt shells, and put them into his bag, along with two more boxes from the shelf. If the hole in the sign was anything to go by, any creature he used the rod against would suffer the same, and it would probably kill it.

His main mission was to get some more metal to make his mirrors with, so he left the building and followed the road a little further into the main town, or what was left of it. Most of the buildings had been flattened in the holocaust, with only the strongest surviving to some degree. Bode was looking for stainless steel, although he didn't know it by that name, as it was the only common metal that stood the test of time without corroding. In places the road was blocked with fallen rubble, which meant a slight detour, and it was on one of these detours that he came across the remains of a 'cookshop'. The building had been reduced to a pile of broken concrete blocks, but glittering in the light of the now descending sun were the remains of many saucepans and other such goods. Bode gathered up as many as he could cram into his already heavy carry bag, and those which would not go in were strung together with cord, and slung over his shoulder.

Bode realised he would have to get his timing right to cross the snake-ridden rocky ridge on his way home, so he decided to spend the night in the first building he had entered that day. On his way back, a dark shape flitted from one pile of rubble to another just ahead of him, and he stopped in his tracks. This was the first sign of life he had ever seen in the ruined city, and it unnerved him somewhat. Was it an animal or another man like himself?

As far as he knew, no one else ever came here, so did others like him live here? He would have to find out for his own safety. Climbing onto a high pile of rubble, he scoured the area ahead, but had to wait some time before he saw the shape again. It looked like a small man, but as it was dressed in rags from head to toe it was difficult to tell. It was certainly furtive in its movements, dashing from one pile of rubble to pause for a while, before hastening to another. As the creature had turned off to the left of the road, Bode thought it safe to carry on towards the building, but he kept a sharp lookout for any other movement in the vicinity.

He reached his haven for the night, and wondered why it still stood while others had been destroyed, not knowing the extra thick reinforced walls of the long gone owner had the foresight to see what might come in the uncertain times ahead, and had taken precautions - but not quite enough.

The door was as he had left it, just slightly ajar, so he thought it safe to enter, using a piece of cord to hold the door shut just in case anything tried to get in while he was asleep, but where would he sleep? The idea of sleeping among the bones of the last occupants didn't appeal to him somehow, so he chose the room of books. The light was fading fast now, and he fancied a hot drink, but a fire in here would soon fill the room with smoke as he couldn't find a fireplace - so he had to make do with some fruit and another bun, along with a drink of water to help it down.

The padded seats of the chairs looked as if they would make something soft to sleep on, but they just crumbled to dust when he tried to remove them. In the end he used a small pile of books to rest his head on, and after a few sneezes from the dust, he fell into a deep sleep.

Because of the low light level in the book room, Bode overslept, which meant the snakes would be active by the time he reached the rock ridge - and that could be dangerous. He hastily ate the last of his fruit, had a drink of water, gathered up his bounty and left the building, putting a small stone against the now closed door of his shelter in case he needed to use it again - if the stone had moved, he would know if something had entered.

He set off up the road leading to the sandy plain and the distant rock ridge as fast as he could, but had to slow down as the scrap metal hanging from his shoulder rattled and clanked, and he was fearful it might attract attention from the rag-covered figure he had seen the day before. The tarmac road ended, and he was out onto the plain where he could speed up, but he was soon out of breath because of the weight of the load.

As the rock ridge came into sight, Bode could see the snakes were already out sunning themselves on the higher rocks, but so far there weren't too many. Did he dare try and get past them? Would they go after him? And what the hell did they eat as there were no other animals around? Would he be on the menu? Although he hadn't seen the giant ones which it was said could swallow a human whole, he didn't doubt they might be there.

Gingerly he began the short climb up the rocks to where it levelled out, and sure enough, there they were, scattered about the pathway, soaking up the rising sun. Fortunately for him they were only small ones, but the sun hadn't reached its zenith yet, and he thought that was when the big ones would come out. Bode thought about fire to scare them off the path, but there was nothing burnable around.

He went back a few metres to where there were some stones on the track and gathered some up, the idea being that if he could make the snakes aggressive, they might attack each other, so reducing the numbers he would have left to deal with. The first few stones went wide of the mark, but then he got the range, and several snakes reared up, and were attacked by those next to them.

The only thing he had with him for protection was his walking stave - he would have to be brave and get closer, and use the stave to hook those which were left in his way off to one side, hoping they wouldn't return before he could get past. The first few he managed to fling to one side were attacked by those they landed on, and then he saw one of the big ones. It was lying curled up on one of the rocks he would have to pass, and as he drew near a pair of steel grey eyes locked onto his.

Without really thinking, Bode flicked one of the smaller snakes just in front of him up into the air and over to land among the coils of the monster on the rock. The reaction was instant - the huge head swung around, the jaws opened and clamped around the head of the smaller snake, and it was drawn down the monster's throat in a few seconds - and then the head swung around to look at Bode again. He flicked two more smaller snakes off to one side, and then a bigger one, and was surprised as to how heavy it was, and then he looked around to see the monster was on the move - in his direction.

He had reached a portion of the track where the downward slope began, and it was in the shade with only one or two snakes ahead of him. He couldn't help it - he ran, or to be more precise, stumbled quickly down the slope, jumping over one of the snakes, and then he was clear of them. He staggered on until he was out of breath and had to stop, with watering eyes and a heaving chest. Bode made a mental note to be very careful in future to get his timing right, and set off for the place by the trees where he had rested before.

He found the water hole he had dug on his outward journey and scooped out two beetle-like things which had fallen in with a few leaves, before slaking his considerable thirst. The water gourds were topped up and some fruit gathered, and he was on his way again after a short rest.

The long trudge across the barren sands was all the more taxing because of the rifle and the amount of metal he was carrying, and he was soaked in sweat by the time he reached the huge cliff and the hole he would have to go down. Picking up the torch which he had left earlier, he lit it with his fire stick, and began the journey down. He was not looking forward to going across the stone bridge as this needed careful balancing, and his load of metal plates and the rifle hanging from his shoulder tended to swing about as he walked.

After careful thought, he decided to split his load and make two journeys across the chasm, which was just as well, as he nearly lost his balance on the second trip.

Once he was out of the dark tunnel and into the open, he could speed up again across the hot dunes, and then as the forest was approached, the sun began its slide down the sky to the time of darkness and he hurried as much as he could to reach the rock he would sleep on that night. In his haste he nearly got caught by a vine he hadn't noticed, and swerved to one side just in time. The huge block of rock was a welcome sight, and he divested himself of his load, leaving it at the base of the rock, only taking up his food bag and some sticks to make a fire.

With the fire lit and merrily blazing away, he felt at ease for the first time on his expedition, but wished he had had the forethought to soak the pot gourd in the water hole, as it had dried out, and he wouldn't be able to make his evening hot drink. The remaining buns were now too hard to bite into, so he had to dribble a little water on one to make it softer and edible, but it still tasted good. He was just dozing off as the lesser sun arose, bathing the forest in its ghostly silver light, and once more he wondered why its light was cold, while the greater sun bathed his world in so much warmth.

Sleeping all night on hard rock made sure he didn't oversleep this time, and he was up early before the greater sun had risen. Climbing down from his lofty perch was made all the more difficult in the half light of dawn, and he was relieved to see his pile of trophies were all intact at the base of the rock where he had left them. Shouldering his load, Bode set off through the forest for the mud pools, noticing on the way that the sleepy flowers had no smell this early in the morning.

He was extra careful negotiating the mud pools, as one slip would be fatal; they also smelt just as revolting as they did in the heat of day. Soon the valley of flying insects was reached, and just in time, as the sun's rays had begun to tinge the top rocks in rose-pink, and they would soon be out foraging.

Bode hardly noticed the rest of the journey home, so pleased was he at what he had achieved. He removed the locking stick from the door, and entered the welcoming coolness of his main living chamber, and sat down with a sigh in his chair.

After resting his tired body for a while, Bode stoked the fire into life, and made himself a hot brew together with a pot of meal gruel. He considered he had done well, as he now had a good collection of shiny metal to make his mirrors, and so go further back into the maze of tunnels and caves he knew to exist behind the small section he used as a home; and he had a formidable weapon, the killing stick, but he would keep that a secret as the elders of the clan would demand he hand it over, and punish him for going into the forbidden lands into the bargain.

CHAPTER 3

BODE MUST HAVE dozed off, for the next thing he knew was a banging on his door. He got up, rubbing the sleep from his eyes and was surprised to see his friend Mel standing there.

"Where have you been? I came yesterday, and the day before and there was no sign of you, and I was about to go away again."

"Oh, I've been doing a bit of exploring," Bode replied, "come in - sorry, I must have been asleep for a while. What brings you here?"

"There's been some murmurings among the clan leaders about you." she said darkly, "They don't think you're really one of us, you never come to the meetings or the ceremonies they hold, and you're always asking them awkward questions when you do see them."

"I don't see any point of going to the meetings," Bode said, with a touch of disdain in his voice, "the silly old farts just mumble on about adding bits to their ceremonies and other inconsequential things which have nothing to do with real life - it's just a waste of time, as far as I'm concerned. Why do you go to them?"

"Well, if I don't," Mel replied, "they may think I'm not contributing to the clan, and not worthy of being a member. A lot of us younger ones feel the same, but don't know what to do about it."

"Well, we could set up a clan of our own," said Bode, "that's if enough of us get together, and let the silly old sods get on with their mumblings. Without the younger members they'd fall apart before long - who's going to do all the work? They don't do anything constructive - just mince about in their robes and tell us off all the time. I'm fed up with it all, that's why I live out here; I can do what I like, most of the time."

"You live out here because your father left this place to you, and from what I hear, they didn't like your father much either - too much of a loner, I think they said."

"So just what's been going on then?" Bode asked, feeling there was more to his friend's visit, "what are they trying to do, expel me?"

"Well, sort of," Mel replied, feeling embarrassed, "I don't think they want any of us to have much to do with you; it's not expulsion exactly, they just want to keep you at a distance, I think. Your ideas are a bit radical, to them that is."

"At least I have some ideas," replied Bode hotly, "so what else don't they like?"

"It's your going into the forbidden lands, they know you do it, and they're afraid you'll bring back some of the evil things the giants made."

"Try and understand this," Bode said, speaking slowly, "the things the giants made are not evil - it's what they did with them that wrecked their world. I only take a few bits and pieces which I think will be useful, like the mirrors I make - all they do is spread light into my home. What's the harm in that?"

"Put like that, I agree with you," Mel said, "I think they're afraid you'll bring back something really evil."

"For God's sake, get this into your head; things are not evil, it's only what people do with them that cause problems." Bode sat back, afraid that if he said any more he would lose his friend.

"I suppose you're right," Mel replied, with resignation, "but they don't see it like that, and that's what worries me - we've been friends for a long time, and I want to keep it that way."

"Have a look at this," said Bode, reaching into his carry bag, and withdrawing a knife, fork, and spoon, "don't these look better than the silly little wooden ones you all use? Where's the evil in these? You couldn't do much with the metal spoon, the fork might leave a few small holes, and the knife could kill, but you would have to want to do that for it to be harmful. So the evil is in the person, not the thing he has. Go on, you can keep them, I've got plenty more." He sat back in his chair, feeling he had made his point.

"They're very nice," said Mel, handing them back to Bode, "but I daren't keep them, someone might see me using them, and tell - they'd guess where I got them from, and then we'd both be in trouble." Bode looked disappointed.

"What are the forbidden lands like?" asked Mel, changing the subject, "I've only heard stories about them."

"Well, they're difficult to get to," Bode replied, "and you have to be careful or you'll get killed on the way. I have only seen a bit of the actual lands, there are lots more to explore. First you see masses of broken buildings, I mean really broken - God knows what could have done that much damage, but in the distance there are tall towers reaching up into the sky - some of them are bent, as though a giant hand had hit them, but some are still upright. I've not been to see them yet, but I intend to, one day. I found one dwelling which was almost intact, and that's where I got these things from. There a lots more things there, but I don't know what they're for, so I left them for now; anyway, my carry bag was full. I really need someone to come with me so I can bring back more useful things."

Mel looked frightened for a moment, fearing she might be cajoled into going on an expedition, and thereby breaking the rules of the clan and what that would entail.

"Will you stay for a meal?" asked Bode, hoping to win his friend over to his way of thinking during the extra time she would be there.

"OK, but I mustn't be late getting back, they'll wonder what's happened to me," Mel replied, remembering that Bode's food was unusual, and often very nice.

They talked on for a while, and then Bode brought out some seed buns and fruit, with a sweet herb tea.

"How come your buns always taste so good, and the fruit is different to ours?" asked Mel, tucking in heartily.

"I make my buns from a different seed to you lot - I get it from up on the plain, just before you go into the flying insects valley, and the fruit comes from the same place. Don't know why you lot don't get it from there - the buns stay edible for days, not like the ones you make."

"We can't go there, you know that," Mel replied, fearing she was going to get caught up in another argument, "it's outside our village boundaries, and it's probably dangerous - that's why we don't go there."

"I've been there many times, and I've survived," Bode replied, "nothing has attacked me so far, and the fruit is so much better there - you really don't have anything to fear, only fear itself, and that load of old nonsense they keep feeding you. Look, you really need to get a grip on things - let me explain; there are three states of existence - there's appearancy, reality, and actuality.

Appearancy is that which appears to be, it just appears to be, but it may not be real. Reality is what you all agree is real, and that may not be real either, but appears to be because you all slavishly believe it to be so. And then there's actuality, that which is really real, like the bun you're eating or the heat from the fire over there. Once you really understand that, you'll see through all the nonsense which holds you all in a sort of slavery - to the so called leaders."

Mel looked quite shocked at Bode's long dissertation, and was beginning to see some sense in it, but it still didn't dispel all her fears.

"OK, suppose I got several of my friends to come here and join you, how could we live? Where would we get our food, and where would we live?" Mel asked, "I doubt they'd let us trade with the rest of the village, so we'd just be outcasts - with nothing."

"You could get your food from the same place I do, and there is plenty of space in my caves until you build your own houses," Bode answered, "all you need to do is get six or so young men who want to come here, with girlfriends who would also like to join, and we could have a new village in no time."

"Who would seal the partnerships?" Mel asked, "the leaders certainly wouldn't come here, and we would all be living in mortal sin."

"Oh, come on," Bode replied, "it's only one man making the bond to a couple, anyone can do that - it's what the couple agree to which really counts."

Mel looked doubtful for a moment, but the ideas were sinking in, slowly.

"OK, I'll see what the others have to say to your ideas," Mel said, after a while of pensive thought, "the leaders won't like it you know."

Bode just grinned; he had taken the first step in setting up a new clan, one which would be based on common sense and an improved lifestyle, if he had anything to do with it. Shortly afterwards, as the greater sun began to dip towards the horizon, Mel left for the village, her head spinning with new ideas and not a little fear of what the outcome would be; Bode meanwhile cleared up the remains of the meal they had just eaten, and noticed the seed stone of one of the fruits they had consumed had split open. In the past he had just thrown them away, but his curiosity was aroused at the split in the stone, and he forced the outer shell open. Inside was a shiny pale brown nut, and he wondered if it was edible. Using a knife, he managed to remove a small flake, and taste it. There was little flavour, but it had an oily feel about it and left a film of oil on his fingers.

Thinking the nut was useless, he threw it into the fire where it promptly burst into flame. An idea was already forming in Bods mind, and using a piece of stick he quickly pulled the nut out of the fire and onto the hearth, where it continued to burn with a slightly smoky flame for several minutes. As there were several seed stones left over from their meal, he stripped the outer shells off them, cut them into flakes and placed the resulting mush between two pieces of wood and put his full body weight on them. A few seconds later, and a thin dribble of oil seeped out onto the stone floor.

Bode scooped up as much of the oil as he could into the small gourd cup, added a piece of his homemade string, and then added a layer of gravel so that the oil was covered and holding the string in the middle of the gourd. The oil soon seeped up the string, and he lit it with a burning twig from the fire.

The oil lamp had just been reinvented.

Bode went into his dark growing room to see how effective the light was, and found it lit the little cave up quite well, once his eyes got used to the low light level - and then he thought "I don't need to make the shiny mirrors now!"

From chance observations and happy accidents come great inventions.

Bode decided that next day he would go and collect all the fallen fruit he could find, save the seed stones, and build up a stock of oil. If the leaders of the clan didn't object, he saw a good trading prospect making oil lamps, but keeping the secret of how he obtained the oil to himself. And then he remembered the stinking mud which went hard when baked in his fire.

There was a little left, but it had hardened somewhat. Bode fashioned a small cup shape with a flat bottom, and then made a lid to fit; the lid had two holes in it, one for pouring in the oil, and a smaller one for the string wick. Moistening the clay, he stuck the lid to the cup and set it by the fire to dry out. That night he would put the 'lamp' in the embers of the fire, and hopefully have a working model of his oil lamp by morning.

Apart from a few dreams of smelly mud pools and angry village elders, Bode had a good night's sleep, and awoke early for a very busy time ahead.

By the time he had finished his first meal of the day, he had devised a method of squeezing the oil from the crushed seed nuts and a new kind of wick for his lamps. He also thought of a new use for the shiny metal; he noticed that when he took his oil lamp into the dark cave he could see better if he shielded his eyes from the flame, so why not put a piece of metal at the back of the lamp so it would act like a shield, and reflect the light forwards?

The first job of the day was to go to the bubbling mud pools to get more clay before the stinging flying insects left their holes, and then on the way back collect as many seed nuts as he could find. By midday he felt exhausted and his arms ached from carrying the heavy loads of mud and seed nuts. The mud was stored in the growing room, and covered with a damp cloth to keep it soft.

Three days later and he had made six oil lamps complete with reflectors, the metal saw he had taken from the giants gun room proving to be one of the most useful tools he now possessed. A nut oil press based on the lever principle got even more oil from the crushed nuts, and he wondered what else might produce oil for his lamps.

Bode was taking a break from his oil production, when Mel paid him a visit.

"So what have you been up to?" asked his friend, "and what are those?" pointing to the little row of lamps. Bode lit one, and gave a demonstration of its effectiveness by taking it into the dark growing room.

"That's amazing," said Mel, "but I don't know what the elders will say about it, they don't like anything new."

"I'm not worried what the elders think, as soon as the rest of the village see how useful they are, they'll want one too - and I am the only one who knows how to make them, and supply the oil, so it looks like we are going to be busy."

"We?" exclaimed Mel, looking worried, "the elders will throw us out of the village, and then what will we do?"

"I doubt it will come to that," Bode replied, "you take a couple of the lamps back with you, and a small supply of oil, and give them to your closest friends. Once word gets around everyone will want one, and then we'll have to go into production. The more people that have a lamp, the more difficult it will be for the elders to put a stop to it - we'll have our own little village in no time. By the way, did you sound out your friends about joining us?"

"Yes, I did," Mel replied, "and quite a few are fed up with present system, so it won't take much to get them on your side - whether they'll join you, I don't know, but I expect some will."

"Good, and now I'll show you something else," said Bode, looking pleased with himself, "one wick gives just about enough light to see what you're doing, so I made a lamp with three wicks, and a reflector."

Bode reached up to a shelf and brought down the three wick lamp, and lit it. Three little flames danced around as he went down the passage leading to the dark growing room, with Mel following close behind.

"Hey, that's much better," exclaimed Mel, impressed, "I bet you could sell that."

"I think for general use, the one wick one lamp is enough, but for exploring the tunnels beyond the section I live in, the extra light is needed - we don't know what's in there."

"You're going in there?" Mel queried, surprised, "I thought you said you didn't dare venture into the old tunnels."

"I did, but that was before I had a good light, going in with fire brands was too risky as they don't last long enough, and as you say, who knows what's in there; now we can go in and find out."

"I notice the 'we' again," said Mel, the worried look returning, "I'm not sure I would want to go in there."

"Whatever is in there has been there for a very long time, so I expect it's dead and therefore harmless," Bode said, "even my so called father said he had never been in there, so I don't think there's anything to fear - are you game to join me?"

"When are you going?" asked Mel, hoping it would be sometime in the distant future, giving her enough time to find an excuse not to go.

"In a few days time," Bode replied, "first you take a couple of lamps back home and see what the reaction is, and if possible get some orders; in the mean time, I'll make some more lamps in case sales take off; then we can go and see what's in those old passages."

CHAPTER 4

Two days later Mel returned, with a bounce in her step and looking much more cheerful.

"Hope you've made some more lamps, I have orders for twelve so far, and four of my friends having seen them want to join us."

"Nice to hear 'us'," said Bode, with a grin, "looks like things are coming together at last. I've made a whole lot of lamps, but oil is going to be a problem. We'll have to go looking for more seed nuts. I think we'll set the price of three tokens for the lamps, and four for a pot of oil. Anything from the elders?"

"So far, not a word; I doubt anyone has shown them the lamps for fear of what they would say, but sooner or later they'll come over here just to see what you're up to."

"I look forward to that day," said Bode, "it's about time some sensible order was brought into the village, even if it's the village we will build here."

"Are you sure about building another village here?" asked Mel, the worried look returning, "who will build it, and where will the materials come from?"

"There's plenty of wood up in the forest, and I have a device much better than an axe for cutting it; stone is no problem, there's lots from the latest cliff fall just up the valley; those who join us will build their own houses, with our help of course."

"I've got one other question," said Mel, "how do you make the lamps? I've never seen a material like it before, is it from the forbidden lands?"

"You must keep this to yourself for now - I found out by accident that the mud from the bubbling pools sets hard when it is dried out and put in my fire, so hard in fact, that it will not go soft again no matter how long I leave it in water - and the smell is gone! Otherwise we wouldn't be able to even give the lamps away. If we get a move on, we'll have time to get some more seed nuts, and there'll still be time for you to get home before the greater sun sinks."

The pair set off for the forest, each taking two large carry bags with them. It was a messy job squeezing the nuts from the fallen fruit, and they had to go some way into the forest to get enough to fill the bags. When they returned, Bode showed Mel how the nut crushing device worked, copious amounts of oil pouring out from the bottom of the contraption and into a series of large gourds Bode had ready.

"You'd best be getting home now," said Bode, "the night flippers will be out as soon as the greater sun dips. They're quite harmless really, but you lot seem to think they're dangerous - those bloody elders will try anything to keep you lot under control."

Mel left with her order of twelve lamps and some gourds of spare oil, thrilled at the prospect of a new life, but terrified of what the elders would make of it, and try to do to stop it.

Bode set to making more lamps, as he was sure they would sell well once word got around, and the lump of clay in the dark room dwindled down to almost nothing. Fed up with making each lamp by hand, he made a mould out of clay, baked it in his fire, and now all he had to do was press clay into the mould and let it dry a little, and a lamp bowl came out; a similar mould was made for the lid with a little spout for the wick to go in, and lamp production was about as mechanised as he was ever going to get it.

Using the three wick lamp, Bode went down the tunnel from his quarters to the section where the heavy wooden door barred any further progress to the mystery passages beyond. He was tempted to try and break down the door on his own, but thought better of it - company was needed on such an expedition, just in case anything went wrong, and he needed help.

Four days later and Mel came rushing in, all flustered and bothered.

"Those lamps sold like hot buns," Mel said, struggling to get her breath back, "I could have sold twice as many, and I now have orders for thirty. Trouble is, one of our elders got his hands on one, wanted to know where it came from, and someone said you. I think they'll be around soon, so you'd better have a good story to tell them if you don't want even more trouble."

"I really don't see what the fuss is about," Bode replied, in all innocence, "all I've done is use local materials to make something useful - none of it has come from the forbidden lands, so what are they so upset about?"

"You know they don't like anything new," Mel responded, "unless it comes from them, but they haven't introduced anything new in my lifetime. Just wait until they hear about your idea of setting up a new village here - they'll explode."

"I think we should be a little subtle about setting up our village. I bet they'll throw us out first of all, just to show their authority. Anyone with a lamp will be under suspicion, so it will only need a few of them to stand up to the elders, and they'll be asked to leave - that way it isn't the villagers leaving, but the elders throwing them out, and that will only make more of them want to leave, especially when they see how good our village is."

"You wily old sod," said Mel, with a grin, "you should have been an elder." Bode just raised his eyebrows, and matched Mel's grin.

Bode got out two gourds and filled them with a pale amber liquid from a larger container, handing one to Mel.

"Try a drop of this," he said, "I thought it a bit of a waste to let all the fruit pulp rot on the ground, so I collected some up and put in the biggest gourd I could find, and left it for a few days. I noticed some time ago that over ripe fruit had a different taste to it, and it was rather nice. This is what's left over when the pulp has finished fizzing. If we can get a few jars of this down the elders throats, it may soften them up a bit."

The pair sat there, sipping away at the fermented fruit juice, and after a couple of refills, the giggling began.

"I can see your point about getting the elders to imbibe in this stuff," Mel said, between chuckles, "I feel almost friendly towards the silly sods."

The cave echoed with laughter as the pair rocked about in their seats, tears streaming down their faces. Soon it was only contented snores which broke the silence of the cave complex, as they both slumped down in their chairs in an alcoholic daze.

CHAPTER 5

It was nearly dark when Mel awoke with a start.

"Hey, wake up Bode, it's got dark, I can hardly see."

Bode stumbled over to the shelf where he kept the lamps, and lit two with a burning piece of wood from the fire.

"My God, I don't want to do that too often," said Bode, shaking his head, and then wishing he hadn't, "I'll bet we could sell that stuff. I think in future we should limit it to one drink only. Looks like you'll have to stay the night, it's too dark for you to make it safely home - we don't know what's wandering about in the dark hours, and the lesser sun will be very small tonight so there won't be much light."

"That's something I've been meaning to ask you," said Mel, "why is the greater sun always the same size, and the lesser one keeps changing size and shape?"

"I don't know - it's always been like that," Bode replied, "I'll bet the giants knew the reason - that's why I want to visit the forbidden lands to try and learn from what they have left behind. They have all sorts of strange things in their buildings, most of which I don't understand, and in one building there are masses of blocks of paper with strange writing on them, and some pictures too - but the paper has rotted over time, and they tend to fall apart if you pick them up."

"Is it like the paper we get from the next village to ours?" asked Mel, "because that doesn't fall apart, but it is expensive to trade for."

"Yes, it's similar, but smoother; I expect they use finer fibres to make it with, not like the wood pulp the other village uses."

"Are you going back there again?" asked Mel, "I'd like to go with you, if it's safe."

"Well, it's safe if you know what you're doing, and take care. There are a couple of scary bits, but I've always managed to make it safely back - it's well worth the risk."

They talked on well into the night, Bode asking Mel if she would help him get some more clay from the bubbling mud pools, but it would mean an early start to avoid the stinging, flying things up in the cliffs. He had thought about making some really big pots from the clay, and towards that end he had built a big fire box a short distance from his home near a wood, as he would need a lot of fuel to fire it.

Next day the pair set off as the lesser sun was about to disappear and a short while before the greater sun burst over the horizon. They were limited to the amount of clay they could carry, but found that if they slung the carry bags on a pole, and put the pole on their shoulders between them, they could bring back just that little bit more.

"Have you thought of looking for the mud nearer your home?" asked Mel.

"There aren't any other mud pools," Bode replied, "but I see what you mean. The mud stuff must be in the ground for the pools to form in the first place, so I'll have a dig around to see if there is any below the surface a bit nearer. If pot production takes off, as I think it will, I don't fancy going all that way to fetch it - good thinking Mel, thanks for that."

They left the valley of the flying things as the first few took to the air, buzzing about above their heads, but they were untroubled by them as Bode had the foresight to make a smoke torch, and lit it just as they were entering the valley on their way home.

"How are you going to make big pots?" asked Mel, as they trudged along, "surely the mud will just slump down into a heap."

"I've already made a small one," Bode replied, "so the same principle should work for a bigger one. I made a flat plate of firm mud for the base, and then rolled out a long snake-like length and stuck it onto the base, winding it round and round and adding more lengths as I went. As long as the mud has stiffened a bit, it stays put. I then work the surface smooth with a flat stick so you can't see the coils. The trick is letting it dry out before I put it into the fire."

The pair were tired by the time they had reached Bode's home, but after the first meal of the day they perked up, and Mel set off for her village carrying the order of thirty lamps she had acquired, and wondering what kind of reception she would get if she met the elders.

Bode spent the rest of the day looking for the red mud to make his pots with, but so far he had little luck, and gave up. In what little light of the day that was left, he set about lamp production, leaving the little row of clay lamps to dry in front of his fire, had a meal, and then spun up the threads from very fine plant fibres to make the wicks, by the light from his three wick lamp.

CHAPTER 6

Two days later at the crack of dawn, Mel came knocking at his door with another order for lamps, a bag of tokens from the lamps she had sold, and news that the elders would be on their way any time soon.

"This should be entertaining," said Bode, with a grin, "you want to stay here to see the fun?"

"You aren't taking this very seriously," Mel replied, looking uncomfortable, "they could cause a lot of trouble for us, as you well know."

"It was going to happen sooner or later," said Bode, "and if we are polite and stand up for ourselves, I don't see what they can do really. Once most people in the village have lamps, they aren't going to give them up easily, so if we play it right the elders will bring about their own demise through their own usual stupidity. Anyway, how many lamps are required?"

"Thirty two, and you'd better put in a few spares; by the time I get back word will have got around even more, and I expect people will want one before the elders put a stop to the supply."

"I've got about forty, and two big pots of oil in store - made them from the same mud stuff as the lamps. I've also made some smaller pots with a wooden bung to hold the refill oil in. You can fill the empty lamps as you sell them from a big pot, and if they want any more oil they can buy a refill pot - we should be rich before long!"

Bode took Mel along to see the wood fired kiln he had made at the edge of the woods, and the huge stock pile of timber he had ready for the next firing.

"If you put a little metal reflector on each lamp you'll run out of shiny metal before long," commented Mel, "and then what will you do?"

"We'll have to make a trip to the forbidden lands to get some more; I want to go there anyway, as there a lot of things I want to see and collect."

By the time they had returned to the cave, the greater sun had risen well above the horizon, and the air was warming up. Mel stuck her head out of the doorway and bobbed back in quickly, saying, "Here comes trouble, two elders and a couple of villagers to keep 'em company."

"Remember, be polite," said Bode, "there's no point in annoying them." and left the door to the cave system open.

"Can we come in," said one of the elders, with a deep authoritative tone to his voice.

They both went to the doorway, bobbed their heads respectfully, and ushered the elders into the main room. The two villagers remained outside, walking about nervously as though they had nothing to do with the visit. Bode offered the two chairs he had in the room, pulling out a bench on which he and Mel sat when the elders had taken their seats.

"We understand you have been supplying a lighting device to the villagers," one of the elders stated, "and without our permission."

"Yes, that is right," Bode replied, calmly, "I didn't know I needed to ask permission to do so."

"Where did you get them from?" asked the other elder.

"I make them," Bode replied, "I thought they would be useful. I needed some light in the time of darkness, and the rush lights don't last very long, so I made these new lights, and very good they are too."

"You should have asked our permission first," said the first elder, putting on a stern face, "they may be evil, and turn our people into evil ways."

"Light is light," Bode replied, "be it from a fire, rush light, the greater sun, or anything else. I don't see how it can be evil."

"How do you know it isn't evil," asked the other elder, "you are not learned in these things, you are only a villager, whereas we have great knowledge on such matters, and that is how we protect our people from harm, and evil."

"I do see your point," Bode replied, "and I'm sorry if I didn't ask your permission first, but let me show you something, and you can then decide if it is evil."

Bode produced a seed nut and cut a piece from it. Placing it on a piece of fired clay, he lit a twig from the fire and took the flame to the piece of nut. It spluttered a bit at first, but then burned with a steady yellow flame.

"Do you consider that evil?" he asked, "it is just a piece of nut, just like the twig I lit it with. It is a natural thing, so there can't be any evil in it, I would suggest."

"We would agree with that," one elder replied, cautiously, wondering where the verbal trap might be, "but that is not the same as the lights you have been supplying the village with."

Bode put a piece of clay on the table, and then added the original hardened piece of clay he found in the fire which had started the whole lamp making business off.

"This is a bit of mud," said Bode, pointing to it, "do you consider that evil?"

"Of course not," replied the first elder, "what are you trying to do, ridicule us?"

"OK, this is a piece of mud which went hard when I put it accidently in my fire," said Bode, trying to keep a calm voice, "it's the same mud, but the heat of the fire has made it hard. So is that evil?"

"Just what are you trying to prove?" replied the elder.

"I am trying to illustrate that natural things are not evil, only what man does with them can cause harm," replied Bode, "If I squeeze the nut, an oil comes out, and that is what burns. The lamp bases are made from that mud, and then filled with the oil. A piece of string is then put into the oil, and it creeps up the string, quite naturally, and when lit it burns, just like that piece of nut. All I have done is take the oil from the nut, put into a container, added a piece of string, and I have a light. What can possibly be evil about that?"

The two elders realised that their argument had been demolished, and tried another line of attack.

"You didn't ask permission to make the lamps," said one, defensively, "and you should have done. Anything new must be approved by us to make sure it contains no evil."

"I didn't want to bother you, as I could see the lamps weren't evil, and it would have taken up some of your time," replied Bode, "and I didn't want to do that and get a telling off for wasting your time. So, may I respectfully ask, do you consider the lamps and the light they give, as evil?"

The elders realised their arguments had been shredded, and both agreed the lamps were not evil, but then tried another tack.

"The dark time is meant for sleeping," one of them said, "so it is against nature to make light to keep people awake when they should be sleeping."

"I would agree with that," Bode replied, "but people already use rush lights, and fire light during the dark time, so should that be stopped as well? Sometimes when the dark storm clouds come over the land, we have to make light, otherwise life couldn't carry on - and anyway, who wants to sleep during the day?"

"We shall take our findings back to the full council," said one of the elders, "and they will decide if you are to be punished, and what that punishment will be."

And with that they both left, somewhat deflated, and very annoyed that a mere villager had got the better of them, and scowling at the two villagers who had now joined them for the journey back.

"Well, that wasn't too bad," said Bode, with a grin at Mel, "a little reasoning and politeness goes a long way."

"I'll bet we haven't heard the last of it," Mel responded, "they won't let you get away with it that easily - and I'm surprised they didn't mention the forbidden lands, they know you go there."

"Which reminds me," said Bode, "we need some more shiny metal for the lamps, so how about you take the latest order back and then return. We can then get an early start as we have to get through the valley of the stinging things before they wake up, through the mud pools and into the forest. We'll spend the night there, it's quite safe, I have a special place to sleep, and then it's off with only one more stop before we reach the forbidden lands - you'll find them really interesting."

Mel left, wondering what kind of reception she would get when she arrived. She needn't have worried, the villagers were only too keen to get their hands on the lamps, and the extra ones were soon snapped up. She returned with another bag of tokens and more orders for lamps. It was obvious that the elders hadn't done anything to stop the inflow of lamps into the village, and if they tried to stop the trade now, it could result in a riot.

CHAPTER 7

L ONG BEFORE THE greater sun broke the horizon, the pair set off for the forbidden lands, Bode in great spirits and Mel a little apprehensive at the thought of the perils which lay ahead.

After their two dark-time stopovers, the forbidden lands hove into sight.

"That must have been a huge village," said Mel, as she looked down on the ruins of the vast city, "I wonder why they destroyed it."

"Don't know, but I'd like to find out", Bode replied, "they must have had great powers, or someone did - but what's the point of destroying everything like this? You wait until you see some of the things they had."

They reached the tarmac road and followed it down to the house Bode had stayed in on his last journey. The stone he had left against the door still there, so he opened it, knowing nothing else had entered since his last visit.

Mel was in awe of the strange things the giants had left behind, and wanted to take everything back with them, Bode reminded her of the main purpose of their visit, but promised to take anything else back if they had the room in the carry bags.

They left the concrete bunker and made their way down the road, climbing over piles of rubble every now and again as the fallen buildings had blocked the road. Bode wanted to reach the area which still had some of the very tall buildings standing, as he felt some of the mysteries about the demise of the giants may lay there.

The first skyscraper they came across had only lost its top, the ground floor seeming to be intact. Gaining access was difficult as the massive doors at ground level seemed to be firmly locked, and there were no windows or other openings. Halfway around the massive structure they came to the goods entrance, and a delivery must have been taking place when the first blast ripped the top of the skyscraper off, and probably killed all those in the vicinity.

"I think we can get in here," said Bode, enthusiastically, "looks like someone has left the doors open."

Once inside, they were surprised how little of the wind blown dust and rubbish had penetrated this part of the building, and then they came to their first pile of bones. Two twisted skeletons lay in a grotesque embrace on the floor, and Mel took a step back with a sharp intake of breath.

"My God, they're so much bigger than us," she exclaimed, "so there really were giants - it's not just old stories."

"I think you'll find a lot of the old stories are based in truth, with bits added by those wishing to scare us half to death. In a way I can see why the elders are so keen for us not to have anything to do with these old artefacts, in case we misuse them and destroy ourselves - but I think they take not using new ideas a bit too far."

They went down the long corridor, opening any door which wasn't locked, and in one storeroom found huge piles of wooden boxes, some of which had been opened. Bode reached into one and withdrew a round tin, on top of which was a pull tab.

"Careful," said Mel, stepping back again, "you don't know what's in there."

"It can't be alive, and it's only a small container," Bode replied, as he pulled on the tab. There was a sharp click, and the lid peeled back. Bode lifted it up to his nose and took a sniff.

"Hey, this smells good, I think it's food of some kind; take a sniff and see what you think."

Mel reluctantly smelt the offered can, and agreed it did smell like food - sort of.

Before Mel could stop him, Bode had dipped a finger into the can and sucked the gravy soaked digit - his face lit up like one of his lamps.

"It tastes a bit like one of those furry little raybits we sometimes catch and cook on the fire, but sooo much better. Come on, try some, it's really good."

"If you haven't blown up, thrown a fit, or turned into some sort of monster by the dark time, I'll try some," said Mel, backing off, "you have no idea of what's in it."

"I think this must be their food store - perhaps they knew something bad was going to happen, and stocked up," said Bode, opening another box, "I'm looking for another container with another picture on it to see if it's different to the first one."

Bode opened the tin of peaches, tasted the juice, and popped a slice into this mouth.

"Must say, their food is so much better than ours. Pity they destroyed everything, we could have done some good trading with them!

I've just noticed something, these containers are made of the same shiny metal I've been collecting - perhaps that's why they have lasted so long, maybe we could use them for cooking in? If we cut the container in half from top to bottom, we'll have two very nice reflectors for our lamps - and no need to hammer the metal into shape. Some of their metal goes a ruddy brown colour, and the surface is all flaky, and of no use, so I wonder why they bothered to use it?"

It was too much for Mel to absorb all in one go, so she just nodded where she thought it was appropriate.

Bode went through the boxes of food, sorting out different tins to sample later, with the intention of emptying some and taking the tins back with them.

"Right, let's see what else we can find," said Bode, striding out along the corridor, "there must be lots of other useful things we can take back."

"But the elders will raise hell if they see them," said Mel, "you know we mustn't go into the forbidden lands, let alone take anything from them."

"Don't see why the elders should see them," Bode responded, "we'll keep them for ourselves and anyone who wants to join us, the elders won't join us, so they won't know."

The next room held materials for making or repairing things, and a good selection of tools; most of which didn't make much sense to either of them, except a series of saws hung on a wall.

"Now these are really useful," said Bode, excitedly, "we can use these."

"What are they?" asked Mel, wondering why Bode was so interested in strips of metal with teeth on them.

"I don't know what they are called, but you can cut wood with them," Bode replied, "I brought one back for the metal on my first visit here, and not knowing what it was for I rubbed a piece of wood against the teeth, and it cut the wood. I think you are supposed to push the blade back and forth across the wood, and it cuts it in two. I know they will be heavy, but we'll take some of them back with us."

The pair explored many other rooms in the base of the skyscraper, but didn't understand what most things were for, except some clothing, but it was too big for them to wear.

"We'll stay here for the dark time," said Bode, "back in the room with the food containers, but first we'll take some of these wood cutting things with us. We must leave early before the greater sun comes up so we can cross the snake ridge before they are awake."

They returned to the storage room, and Bode set about opening up two cans of meat stew and then some from the tinned fruit box. Finding a few pieces of wood which had survived the long time from the holocaust, he lit a small fire, and stood the two cans of stew on the embers. The smell was too much for Mel, who edged closer and closer to the dying fire, and when Bode took a can, she did likewise. Soon the only sound in the building was that of slurping, and a low moaning sound from the wind as it threaded its way through the ruined top of the skyscraper.

"Well, how was that?" asked Bode, when Mel eventually put down the empty can, "I'll bet you've never tasted anything like that before. Now try the fruit, it's delicious. When we've finished our meal, I would suggest we empty as many of these containers as the carry bags will hold, with a few full ones for when we get home, and then we will be ready for an early start."

Bode added a bit more wood to the embers, and they sat there in the flickering fire light for a while, talking over their plans for the future. Finally, tiredness took its toll, and they both curled up for the night by the glowing embers, their only fear was of not waking up early enough next morning, but they needn't have worried, Mel's snores brought Bode awake just as the lesser sun was sliding down towards the horizon. There was just enough light coming in through the reinforced window for him to see by, so he awoke Mel - who was none too pleased at the disturbance to her dreams.

The carry bags and a selection of saws were loaded onto a long pole slung between them, and they set off in the silvery light for the long trek home. The pair cleared the snake ridge just as the greater sun peered over the distant hills, tingeing them in a blaze of red and yellow, and then the long journey across the desert began.

With a stopover for the dark time on Bode's rock pile in the forest, and they were nearly home, although negotiating the mud pools with their heavy load frightened Mel more than she admitted.

Arriving back at the cave, there was a reception committee waiting for them. Four young men stood around the cave door, looking very fed up, and not a little scared.

"We thought you'd gone for good, or been eaten by that new creature roaming about the area - where have you been?"

"On a very long journey," said Bode, "and we're totally whacked. Let's get this stuff inside, and we'll attend to you."

The pair were relieved to get the heavy load off their aching shoulders, and the bounty from the forbidden lands was carried into the cave complex by many willing hands.

Bode relit his fire and made a brew of herb tea which was handed around to the other four, and then he asked them why they were here.

"We've been thrown out of the village," said one, "and we came here because Mel said you might start up another village."

"How come you got thrown out?" asked Bode, half knowing what might have happened.

"The elders came around asking for the lamps; some people gave them up, but we refused, saying that we had paid for them and they made life easier in the dark time. A bit of an argument started, and the elders said we were no longer members of the village, and would have to leave, as no one would have anything go do with us now - so here we are. Are you really going to start another village?"

"If another village is needed," said Bode, "then we'll start one. There's plenty of building material here, stone just up the valley and plenty of timber in the forest to cut down and build with - that's if you don't mind a bit of hard work."

"I don't think we have an option," one of the four said, "but what few tools we have for building are back in our village, how can we cut wood without axes?"

"Don't worry," said Bode, "we have much better tools than the village, and it won't take long to build new houses. We'll build one first, which you all will have to share, and then as others are assembled you can invite some of the young girls to join you - we'll have a new community in no time, and once the other people see what we have, they'll want to join us."

The four visitors looked relieved as they supped their herb tea, the idea of being free of the interfering elders appealed to them, and they said so.

"Are you going to be our new elder?" asked one of them.

"I am not an elder," said Bode, "I can give you good advice and help you, but it's up to you as to whether you take it. I have learned a lot by living on my own away from your village and the nonsense of the elders, and I survive very well. I can see some things from the elder's point of view, they believe the old stories which have been passed down through the generations, but they haven't applied any common sense to them to see if they are really true - I have, and most of it is nonsense, designed to keep you all in fear. The elders have a good life, but they don't contribute to the village, everyone has to wait on them hand and foot and all they actually do is lord it over you all."

"Someone said you go into the forbidden lands, against the orders of the elders," one of the visitors said, hesitantly, "why do you do that when you know it's dangerous?"

"It's not dangerous," Bode replied, "we have just come back from there, and no harm has come to us. We bring back things which are useful, things which will help us survive better. The elders don't want you to go there in case you realise the truth, and therefore no longer obey them. The forbidden lands were once inhabited by people just like us, but a bit bigger, and for some reason we don't understand, destroyed themselves a long time ago. As I have said many times, things don't harm people, it's what they do with them that causes harm."

By midday, they were all talked out, and Bode suggested they set about building the first house. He had already planned out where the new village should be constructed, near a stream so that all would have fresh water, and in a circle so that they would have a sense of community.

With six of them hauling stone, the outline of the first house was soon assembled, and the walls began to grow. It was a simple construction of two main rooms with space to add more as time and necessity demanded. When Bode brought out the saw to fell trees, and brought one down in minutes, the four newcomers were very impressed. He told them where he had got it from, and about some of the other wonders to be had there, not that they understood everything, but they showed interest.

By evening time the basic walls were complete, and the first of the roof trusses were in place. After a meal prepared by Mel, they all retired to the main cave, lit by several of Bode's lamps, with the fire burning merrily in its alcove.

"These buns are great," said one of them, "why don't we have buns like these?"

"Because I use a different grain to that used in the village; I have told the elders about it, but they won't allow it to be collected - God knows why, just part of their strange ways, I suppose."

Talk went on well into the dark time, with a small gourd of Bode's special fermented drink being given to each. They all slept well that night, despite the hard cave floor for the four newcomers.

Next morning, they had two more young men asking to join them; they too had been asked to leave the village after an altercation with the furious elders about handing over their lamps, and said discontent was spreading fast.

With eight eager pairs of hands at work, the first house was finished that day. The roof, unlike those of the old village which were covered in grass and had to be replaced frequently, was clad in long wooden shingles, split from sections of tree trunk, and held in place with wooden pegs.

The introduction of Bode's hand drill while roofing, which he had acquired from an earlier visit to the ruined city, caused a sensation among the newcomers. It reinforced Bode's statement that not all things made by the giants were bad.

With the drill and a selection of saws, crude furniture for the first house was made, and the first occupant moved in. He had a wooden bed just about big enough for two, a table and two benches, and a cupboard to store food in. A fireplace in one wall with a side oven would be enough for simple cooking, and baking the staple buns.

Quite a celebration was held that night, with another round of Bode's fermented brew to end the evening. Next day they would have to go out for more fallen fruit to make the next brew, and the seed nuts for oil.

When word got back to the village of how the new settlement was getting on, three more young men joined them. They also brought more news of the large animal roaming the area; it had attacked one of the villagers and eaten him. The elders had held a prayer meeting, and blamed the lamp users for bringing this new evil into their community, but not everyone was convinced that the lamps were the cause. According to one young man, when the villagers heard the elders were on one of their 'lamp seeking' manoeuvres, everyone hid their lamps.

CHAPTER 8

As THEIR NUMBERS grew, house building speeded up, and soon there was a neat circle of houses with a village green in the middle. Everyone agreed it was much better than the old village. Most of the men had already mentioned to their partners their intent to join Bode before leaving the old village, so it didn't take much persuading for them to join the new settlement. Once the circle of new houses had been completed, a new outer circle was begun, with a wide grass band between the two. Neat paths of gravel linked the houses into a harmonious whole, unlike the earthen paths of the old village, which turned to mud in wet weather.

Mel led several journeys into the forbidden lands, bringing back many useful tools and supplies of tinned food, which was enjoyed by all. There were now plenty of oil lamps to go round; and every now and again, someone from the old village would sneak out to purchase a lamp, and smuggle it back.

Bode was amazed at how quickly the new settlement had grown, and how the old fears and beliefs had faded into the background. He had assumed leadership by default, and had some trouble in stopping the new group members from asking his permission to do the simplest of things. Once free of the shackles imposed by the old elders, he found members of the settlement enjoyed experimenting with things, as he had done, and encouraged it.

Trips to the forbidden lands became more frequent, and new tools and materials flowed into Bode's village, enhancing life for all. And then came news that the carnivorous animal roaming around the old village was getting bolder as it met no resistance to its forages. In desperation, one of the old villagers came to Bode asking if he could help them drive it away. It was then that Bode remembered the 'killing stick' he had brought back from the forbidden lands, and offered his help.

Next day Bode and Mel set out for the old village with the rifle and a full clip of ammunition, to be greeted by five elders and about twenty villagers, all armed with pointed sticks. Bode explained that the device made a loud noise when used, and not to be afraid of it. Before he could do anything else, one of the elders stepped forward and accused Bode of using the evil tools of the giants, and would be punished accordingly. Much to his surprise, the elder was shouted down by the angry villagers, and they asked him if his device could actually kill the monster.

The whole group moved back into the village, and scouts were sent out to try and locate the animal which was causing so much havoc. It was midday before anyone saw it, and came running back to inform Bode. He had previously cut a pole with a vee section on its end to support the heavy rifle, as without it the rifle wobbled about too much for an accurate shot.

With Bode in the lead, and the rest of the villagers well behind, he went to the area where the animal had been seen, but there was no sign of it. Bode thought it might have snatched its meal and retired to eat it in comfort, and then it appeared around one of the buildings - it was huge, and Bode wondered if the killing stick would be enough to stop it. As Bode hadn't run away, the creature stopped in its tracks - this was something new to it. Bode propped the end of the rifle on the supporting stick, lined up the sights and squeezed the trigger.

The discharge made his ears ring, and for what seemed like a few seconds the creature just stood there, and then dropped in a crumpled heap, a neat hole in its head spurting blood. When the others realised the creature was dead, a great cheer rang out and there was much back slapping.

"Where there is one of these, there is likely to be more," Bode announced, "so be on the lookout for others, and come tell me if you see one."

"You have used one of the evil devices of the giants," one of the elders shouted out, "and will be punished!"

"Oh shut up," Bode responded, "you don't know what you're talking about."

That was all that was needed for the rest of the villagers to vent their anger on the elders with a tirade of insults and curses. Bode knew the end of the ruling elders was fast approaching.

A few days later a small group of older people from the old village came calling, asking if they too could join the new settlement. Mel showed them around, and they were astonished at the new houses which had been built with their shingled roofs.

"They're so much nicer than ours," one of them said, "and they look so pretty."

"If you want to join us, you will have to give up your old ways and superstitions," said Mel, "we don't stand for any of that old nonsense here - not now since we have discovered the truth about the giants and their demise. What your elders told you is untrue, and caused a lot of unnecessary fear."

"Some of us have realised that for a while," an old man said, "but we didn't know what to do about it."

Within ten days, just about all the inhabitants of the old village had asked to join the settlement, with the exception of the elders, and Bode wondered if some of them would have liked to come too. This new influx meant most houses had to double up, until new homes could be built; but as the building crew had become quite skilled at house construction, it didn't take long for everyone to be allocated a new home.

53

CHAPTER 9

ONE DAY MEL asked Bode if he had forgotten about the old sealed tunnels behind his living quarters.

"No, I've not forgotten, just been a bit busy," Bode replied, "I intend to explore them soon, everything seems to be taking care of itself at the moment."

Each group of ten houses was asked to choose someone to represent them on the settlement council, and so came about a governing body to oversee the whole new village. Bode was asked to head this group, but he politely declined for the time being as he still had a lot of work to do, but he would consider it in the future.

At last the time for tunnel exploration came. Bode told one of the council of his intentions in case he got trapped therein, so help could be sent if he didn't return in a few days.

With their triple lamps lit, a stock of food and drink, spare oil and his fire stick, Bode and Mel set off down the tunnel at the end of his quarters to be confronted by the massive wooden door. Not only was it locked, but large battens of wood had been fixed across it, which had to be prised off. They couldn't see how the lock worked, so brute force was used to smash it off, and the door swung open together with a gush of stale air.

"This place must be very old," said Mel, wrinkling up her nose, "do you really think it's worth going on? The tunnel walls are very rough and jagged, so I doubt it was made by the giants."

"Let's see what's at the end of it," Bode replied, "we may be in for a surprise - it's just a feeling I have."

They walked on down the rough hewn tunnel until they came to a metal door blocking their way, with strange writing on it in big letters.

"These marks look like those in a ruined building I visited in the forbidden lands," said Bode, "there were thick blocks of paper with those sort of markings on them, much like the pictures we make to represent things, I wonder what it means."

"Maybe it's an instruction to do something," said Mel, "but what happens if we do the wrong thing?"

Just then, as the couple moved closer to the door, there was a loud click, the door opened, and they stood facing a small square room with a box-like structure against one wall. Suddenly a light came on, or to be more precise, the whole area gently glowed, dimming their oil lamps.

"Greetings - do not be afraid - this is a recorded message - there is no one here but you. Please listen carefully to what I have to say - I will explain what you have found, and what it means to your future. You have found The Depository, a place where we have put things which will be useful to you and the future of our race.

"A very long time ago, the three most powerful nations of the World were armed with mighty weapons - so great were they that if war started it would most likely kill everyone - we all lived in great fear of this happening. There were two main types of weapon, the hydrogen bomb which would destroy whole cities and the areas around them, and the neutron bomb which is not so destructive, but exterminates all life with its deadly rays.

"Tension had been building for a long time between the nations, and we, a group of scientists, have constructed this store of the most important things we think you will need to survive.

"At the other end of the cliff from where you are now, we built an Ark, a place of safety where a number of people could survive if the war started; it is stocked with food and all other necessities. Power is supplied by a fusion generator which will last for five months. At the end of this time, the ark will open, and you, the occupants will be released out into the world. The areas destroyed by the hydrogen bombs will remain radioactive for a very long time, and you must not go near them because the deadly radiation will make you ill - and in time will kill you.

"The areas where the neutron bombs have landed will be clear of radiation in a few months, and it will be safe for you to go there.

"Once the Ark had been constructed to house a certain number of people, a geneticist discovered that the number was too small to provide a sustainable breeding stock without genetic defects. There wasn't time to enlarge the Ark as things were reaching a critical state between the nations - the only solution to this problem was to seek out smaller people that could be housed in the same space.

"For you to have got this far, we estimate you must be those people, or the descendants of them, but to make sure that you are, there is one more thing you must do to verify this.

"There is a box on the wall with six levers on it. When you hear the tone, you must push lever number one, four and five down at the same time. If you do this, the next door will open and you will have access to The Depository, which has many rooms in it. There is a learning machine there which will teach you how to write and read - just follow the verbal instructions. You will need to be able to read so that you can understand the information we have gathered for you, and how to make the things you will need.

"There is a huge stock of materials to make things with, and instructions on how to replenish the stocks before they are all used up.

"When you enter The Depository there will be a short wait as the fusion generator starts up and the lights come on. When you leave, the generator will go into sleep mode to save power and switch on again when you come back - we think it has enough fuel to last for about five to seven years.

"We wish you well, and hope that in time you will multiply enough to populate the World again, but please do not make the same mistakes our leaders did, and destroy everything.

"You have one minute before the tone sounds, and then you must push down the correct levers. This message and explanation can be heard again once you are inside The Depository - go to the tall box just inside the door, and press the green button."

"So that's why we're smaller than the people who built this place," said Bode. "I knew there must be some explanation."

"And that's why we mustn't go into the forbidden lands," added Mel, "so does that mean we will die?"

"No, I don't think so," Bode replied, "I've been going there for some time, and I haven't been ill. Perhaps we didn't go in far enough to where these bomb things were. So what do we do now? Are you game to go in? - it seems we can go in and out again if we want to, I don't think any harm will come to us."

"We've come this far," Mel said, "so let's do it - but we'll have to wait for the tone, whatever that is."

Just then a single musical note sounded, and Bode stepped forward to the line of levers, positioned his fingers over the correct ones, and pressed down. There was soft clink from somewhere inside the box, and the huge door swung open - to blackness.

A series of sounds followed, whirring, clicks, and a soft hum from somewhere deep inside the room. Slowly the lights came on, and they were amazed at the size of the place. All along the walls were benches full of tools and other strange pieces of machinery, viewing screens, (although they didn't know what they were at the time) and the walls themselves were covered in pictures showing what the old World had been like before the great destruction.

The pair wandered from bench to bench, recognising some things, but totally mystified about others, and then they found the passage leading to the other rooms.

The pair thought the first room was for teaching, as it had a big screen on the wall and in front of the screen was a semicircular row of chairs. There was enough seating for ten people, and the height of the seat was obviously meant for people smaller than the giants. Mel was all for sitting down to see what would happen, but Bode wanted to see what else the complex held.

Another room, of huge proportions, held rods, bars, tubes, and sheets of metal and some other materials which they didn't recognise in giant racks along the walls, and at one end were various machines for cutting the materials.

"Just think of all the trouble we went to in order to get a few bits of that shiny metal, when there was a mass of it so close by," said Bode. Mel said nothing as she was still in awe of the whole place, trying to make sense of so much alien material and equipment.

They went from room to room, gazing in wonder at all the strange machines and other equipment on display, and totally overwhelmed at the size of The Depository.

"I wonder what the others in our group will make of all this," said Bode, "I think we'll have to give a few talks first to get them used to the idea of what has happened."

"It'll take more than a few talks," Mel replied, "this lot will frighten the life out of them, I know it would me if I saw it for the first time. We've been in here quite some time, don't you think we should go back to the others in case they come looking for us and find all this?"

"Yes, good idea; I got carried away by it all, there's so much to see. We'll have to work out some way of getting them used to the idea of what happened, and then introduce them to it in small groups. But first we'll have to undo all the nonsense they've picked up from the elders."

They returned to the main entry door, Bode wistfully looking back at all the wonders on display, and then pushed the door closed. Back in his main room Bode stoked up the fire and made a hot drink, while Mel went to tell the councillor that they had returned safely, and Bode would tell him what they found later.

"I think the best thing to do is to get the whole lot of 'em together one evening," said Bode, "unravel the crap the elders have been spouting for years, and then gently break the news of what really happened. We shall then have to take groups of ten at a time and help them to learn about reading with the machine - but we'll have to get used to it first. It's important to stay one step ahead of everyone else to give them confidence in us."

The meeting of the whole village was set up to take place in two days time, where they would assemble on the central green when the greater sun was halfway down to the horizon, it being a bit cooler then, and giving Bode enough time to tell his tale before it got dark.

Mel reckoned that most of the old village had now joined them, except for the elders and a few who didn't like change, but word had got out to the other village, and they were now making enquiries about joining the new outfit.

CHAPTER 10

THE DAY OF the great meeting came, and Bode began to feel a little bit nervous about it.

"If I don't get it just right I can see the whole thing falling apart at the seams," he told Mel, who assured him that she would back him all the way, and anyway, the whole thing was self-evident if you had more than two brain cells to rub together.

The whole village gathered on the green, and a small podium had been built at Mel's instruction so that all assembled could see and hear the speaker that bit better. Mel introduced the speaker in a rather formal manner as the leader of the community, indicating that he would announce some very important information which would change all their lives - this brought a stunned hush to all those assembled, and all eyes turned to a rather nervous Bode who mounted the podium, cleared his throat, and began.

"Thank you for attending. I have some information for you all which some may find hard to believe. All I ask is that you listen and think about it before making up your minds as to whether you think it is true or not.

"First the elders. In the beginning, I'm sure their intentions were honourable and true, but over time the stories they told became corrupted, bits forgotten and other things added, mainly to increase the power they hold over you. You do all the work and live in fear of them and the threats they issue, while they live a life of luxury and do nothing to help or advance our wellbeing. They tell you that the forbidden lands are evil and will kill you if you go there - it's not true, Mel and I have been there and brought back some of the things the giants made, and we are still alive. Some parts are dangerous, but the parts we have been in are quite safe. Why didn't they want you to go there? Because you might find out the truth, which we have, and then they would lose control over you all. You have seen the rod like thing I killed the creature with, which was killing some of you. The elders did nothing to protect you, but the fire rod I used came from the forbidden lands, and that got rid of the creature.

"I must now give you a bit of history - from the beginning of the troubles the giants experienced.

"A very long time ago, the giants ruled the world, and they were in three main groups. There were millions of them, and for some reason they fell out, and a war was about to happen between them. Their weapons were such that if used it would destroy all the people and their houses - everywhere.

"Some of the giants were good people, and didn't want a war but they couldn't stop it, so they built an Ark, a place where some could live and survive the war, and then come out to start all over again. They chose the smallest people so that they could get in as many as possible. After the war ended, the small people came out - and we are the descendants of those people.

"We have discovered a special place where the giants have left us some of the things they made, to help us progress and lead a better life, and not to make the same mistake they did. In this place is a learning machine which will teach you to read, and then you will be able to understand how their machines work, and how to make things for ourselves. You will be able to read their books - books are a bit like the paper we make to draw symbols of things on, except there are many pages to their books.

"Do any of you have any questions?'

"Why couldn't the good people stop the bad people from going to war?" someone asked,

"I don't know the answer to that, but I'm sure the books will tell us," answered Bode.

"Why did they make such terrible weapons?" another asked.

"That too will be revealed if you read the books," Bode said.

"What do we do about the elders?"

"We don't have any elders here, they didn't want to join us," Bode answered, "we just leave them where they are. If they want to come here they will have to give up their bad ways and contribute to the village. To prevent more elders from starting up, I have set up a council, a member from each group of you to help run the village. If you think the member is doing bad things, he can be stood down, and another elected, that way we protect ourselves from any one person or group taking control away from us, the people."

"Do we have to go into the forbidden lands to learn to read, and use the machines?"

"No, the reading machine in hidden in the back of my cave system, along with a supply of materials to use. I have only just found it - I think it was hidden there until we reached a time when we wouldn't misuse it," said Bode.

A low hubbub of voices slowly rose to a point where Bode could hardly hear himself speak, and he had to wave his arms about to get their attention and quieten down.

"In a few days time, we can begin the reading lessons. I would like you to make up groups of ten people, a mixture of men and women, as the teaching room can only take ten at a time. Each group will have a number so that they can leave off for a while if they want, while another group has a go. That way, the machine will know when you enter your number, and it will begin again where you left off last time. If you would like to make up your groups and elect a leader for each group, that person will be responsible for getting you together when it is your turn, and can report back to me if you have any problems. Thank you for listening; I hope it wasn't too much to take in, all in one go, but if you have any questions, you can come to my cave each time the greater sun gets low in the sky, and I will try to help. Thank you."

A few hand claps began, with the odd cheer, and then it quickly rose to a sound like thunder, echoing back from the cliff, and sending a tingle down Bode's spine.

"My God, you've started something now," said Mel, giving Bode a slap on the back, "I only hope we can keep up the pace with the learning machine - remember, we must keep one step ahead, as you said earlier."

"I think we'll start tomorrow, I've had enough for one day," Bode replied, "and the greater sun is sinking - time for some refreshments."

They retired to Bode's main room, stoked up the fire, and waited for the water to heat up to make a herb drink. Neither slept very well that night - nor did the rest of the village.

Next day, after a quick meal, the pair went into the teaching room and sat down in the chairs facing the screen, but nothing happened.

"Perhaps we have to do something to start the thing off," said Mel, "or maybe all ten have to sit down at once."

Bode was just about to get up and inspect the bench in front of the screen for some means of kicking the thing into action, when the speaker sounded a 'ping'.

"It has been detected that only two persons are seated - do you wish to begin?"

"Yes please," said Bode, without thinking, and then feeling foolish for speaking to a machine.

"Below your chairs you will find a skull cap attached to a wire. Place the cap on your heads - it will help you to retain that which you will see and hear - this system has been use for a long time to teach our children, and is very helpful. It is thought that by the time you hear this you my have lost the art of reading."

With the skull caps on, the pair sat back, and the teaching began. First they learnt about numbers, and how they were constructed and what they meant. Then the alphabet and how the letters made up words. Words, and pictures of what the words meant flashed across the screen in fast succession, far faster than they realised at the time.

"It is suggested you now take a break from learning. Please enter a number on the pad before you, so that teaching can continue when you are next ready - this will be your personal number, so remember it for the future - thank you."

"Funny," said Bode, "I didn't notice a number pad before, we'll call ourselves number 1." And he entered the number on the keypad.

"Thank you" said the screen speaker, and then shut down.

"I'd like to look at a book," said Mel, "just to see if it works - this teaching stuff."

They went into the library and Mel took down a book from the shelf.

"My God, I can read - I understand what it says," Mel exclaimed, with a look if shock on her face, "but there are some words I don't understand."

"Let me have a go," said Bode, taking the book. A pause, and then, "That bloody machine really works, but like you, there are a few words I don't understand - they are just a jumble of letters. Maybe it hasn't shown us all the words yet."

They left The Depository and returned to Bode's main room, both with raging thirsts and hungry.

"Hey, the greater sun is on the way down," said Mel, peering out of the small hole which passed for a window, "we must have been in there for a lot longer than we thought."

As the sun dipped even lower towards the horizon, Bode noticed a little queue of people assembled outside his door.

"Looks like we've got some question to answer," he said, "I don't really feel like it just now, but we started this, so we'd better get on with it."

Most of the questions were simple enough, but a few even Bode couldn't answer, saying the teaching machine would probably solve their queries. By the time they had finished they were both ready for bed, had a light meal, and retired for the dark time.

The following morning, it was back in the teaching room with the skull caps on, their identifying number keyed in, and the second session was under way. At long last the end of the reading lesson was reached, and the machine told them so.

"Thank you for your time. You have now finished the reading lessons. Writing lessons can be started when you wish - just enter your number. Later you may need instruction on using some of the machinery - just enter your number and select the required item from the screen."

"They've thought of everything, by the look of it," said Mel, in admiration, "I would have liked to have met these people, the good ones must have been wonderful to know."

"I agree," said Bode, "but now we are to replace them in this world - I only hope we can do a good a job of it."

Over the next few days, groups of ten villagers went into the teaching room and came out more than amazed. Once they had got used to reading, the hunger for the books surprised Bode, and he had to organise a system of booking out and in the books from the library, so that none got lost in the reading frenzy.

Cal, one of the first people to seek sanctuary in Bode's new village, came to him one day with a proposal.

"I've been reading one of the books on electricity," he said, "the stuff The Depository runs on, and I reckon I could make it for the houses in the village. Then they could have better light. There's a waterfall at the end of the cliff, and if we run a pipe from the top, the water pressure could drive a wheel and that would run a generator - so producing electricity."

"That sounds like a good idea," said Bode, "but what would you use to make the light?"

"I've been in one of the stores, and there is a huge amount of wire and those long clear tubes, like the ones giving light in the rooms there. I've been through all the books on the subject, and I reckon I could do it, with a little help."

"OK, but we must be careful not to use up all the materials they have left us," Bode replied, "until we can replace them - but go ahead, it might spur others on to make things. One other thought, there may be a lot of things we can bring back from the forbidden lands which haven't been destroyed; see if you can get anyone interested in making one of those steam powered things on wheels shown in the books, I know they were only used in their early days, but we don't have the special oil stuff they did for their more modern engines. Then we can collect anything useful that is still intact."

After a lot of trial and error, Cal got his lighting system up and running, allowing one light tube per house, but this reduced the stocks

of tubes so they set about finding out how to make them themselves -
but this would take a long time to perfect.

Once new things were made and distributed among the villagers,
things took off at a great rate, everyone wanted to be in on the act. The
wood burning steam driven cart was a success beyond their wildest
dreams, and a new way around the mud pools and snake ridge was
found. Soon materials from the forbidden lands were flooding in, and
safely, once someone had found the Geiger counter, and learned how
to use it.

By the time Bode and Mel had reached old age, a system of justice
had been established, laws and rules for the good of all were in place,
and the population had grown to huge numbers. Once more, mankind
began its march across the shattered world of the ancients, this time
determined not to make the same mistakes.

THE END

*If you have enjoyed this book, please consider leaving a review on
Amazon. It would mean a lot to us.*

About the Author

"Back in 1998 I was commenting to a friend that I didn't go much on so called modern Science Fiction. It didn't seem as good or as interesting as the adventures stories written by the old masters of sci-fi – Clarke, Russell, Pohl, Asimov, Heinlein etc. His reaction was 'well, write your own then' – As I already had an idea at the back of my mind, I did. After printing up ten copies and binding them (hardback) they were passed around among like minded friends – and then came the request for more of the same! Again and again. Only one problem – I was spending too much time printing and binding and not writing, which I enjoy. Getting into 'print' is difficult – if not impossible – so I chose the 'eBook' route. I would recommend it to anyone who likes writing, and has a story to tell."

David (aka D.B) Reynolds-Moreton is a retired research and development engineer who lives in Devon, England with his wife. You can read a short biography of his life and adventures in science at :

www.sci-fi-cafe.com/david-reynolds-moreton